E   Daly, Catherine
DALY

THE WAY I FEEL TODAY

DATE DUE	BORROWER'S NAME	ROOM NUMBER

The Way
I Feel Today

by Catherine Daly
illustrated by Tom Brannon

Simon Spotlight

New York   London   Toronto   Sydney   Singapore

Based on the TV series *Bear in the Big Blue House*™
created by Mitchell Kriegman. Produced by
The Jim Henson Company for Disney Channel.

 SIMON SPOTLIGHT
An imprint of Simon & Schuster Children's Publishing Division
1230 Avenue of the Americas
New York, New York 10020
Manufactured in the United States of America
First Edition   10 9 8 7 6 5 4 3 2 1
ISBN 0-689-83454-3

Bear woke up bright and early. He yawned and stretched. "What a beautiful morning," he said. "Today is going to be a great day. I feel very excited!"

After breakfast, Bear went outside to check the mail. Inside the mailbox was a nicely wrapped package. "It looks like it's for Pip and Pop," Bear said.

Pip and Pop stood in the doorway, waiting for the mail. They were jumping up and down. "Open it, Bear, open it!" they said.

"What's so special about this package?" Bear asked.

"Well, Bear, we sent away for something that will change our lives forever," Pop explained.

"Wow!" said Bear. "I wonder what it is." He tore open the box and pulled out . . . a clam.

Bear was puzzled. "Uh, guys," he said.

"Yes?" said Pip.

"This is a clam. I thought you already had plenty of clams."

"We do," said Pop. "But this isn't any ordinary clam, Bear."

"It's Clammy, the talking clam. It's the best talking clam toy in the whole world!" the otters said together. They pushed the button on top of the clam.

Clammy laughed a crazy laugh and said, "Is it cold in here, or am I just Clammy? I'm Clammy!"

Pip and Pop roared with laughter.

"Wow," said Bear. "You guys are sure having a good time. You're so happy! Being happy is a great feeling. In fact, it's my favorite feeling of all."

Pip and Pop went off to play with their new toy.

Feeling happy himself, Bear sat down on the couch to read a book. All of a sudden, he heard a crash.

"Oh, no!" cried Pip and Pop.

Bear found the two otters at the kitchen table with Clammy. "Speak to us, Clammy!" they cried.

"What happened?" asked Bear.

"Oh, Bear," said Pip. "We were just sitting here . . ."

"And I guess we got a little carried away," continued Pop, "because the next thing we knew, Clammy was on the floor."

Pip and Pop began to cry.

Just then Bear spotted some batteries on the floor. "Hey, guys, look at these!" he said, picking them up. "Clammy's not broken after all. His batteries just fell out when he dropped onto the floor." Bear popped the batteries back in. "Now he should be as good as new."

Nervously, Pip and Pop pressed Clammy's button.

Clammy laughed his crazy laugh. "Hey, I used to be shy," Clammy said. "But now I've come out of my shell!"

"Yay!" cheered Pip and Pop. "Clammy's back! Thanks a lot, Bear!"

"Come on, Pop," said Pip. "Let's show Clammy to Big Old Bullfrog out at the otter pond."

"Wow," Bear said to himself. "When they thought Clammy was broken, Pip and Pop got really sad. And now they're happy again. Feelings change all the time."

Bear thought for a moment. "What should I do now? Should I take a bath or a nap?"

Suddenly he heard a loud "Whoops!" It was coming from upstairs.
"Oh, no! Ojo!" Treelo cried.
"I bet Ojo and Treelo could use my help," said Bear.

Ojo was by the bedroom window, holding an empty box. Treelo looked very angry.

"What's wrong?" Bear asked.

"Ojo lose Treelo feathers!" said Treelo.

Ojo tried to explain. "I was just playing with them and . . . ," she began.

But Treelo wouldn't let her finish. "Treelo very mad at Ojo! Treelo leave!" He stomped out of the room.

"Ojo, why don't you tell me how this happened?" Bear asked gently.

Ojo sighed. "Okay, well, we were playing with Treelo's feathers . . . and I kind of . . . knocked the box and they went out the window. But it was an accident," she said. "What if Treelo never wants to be my friend again?"

"Being worried isn't a very good feeling, is it?" Bear asked.

Ojo shook her head sadly.

"Why don't we find Treelo?" suggested Bear. "I think you should tell him what happened."

Bear and Ojo found Treelo by the otter pond.

"Treelo, I know you're angry right now," Bear said, "but if you listen to what Ojo has to say, I don't think you'll be mad anymore."

"No. Treelo want to be angry forever!" Treelo announced.

"I don't think you'd like being mad forever," Bear said. "You couldn't jump and laugh anymore, or swing in the trees like you do when you're happy."

"No swinging?" asked Treelo.

"Nope. You couldn't be happy *and* mad at the same time, could you?" Bear asked.

Treelo thought hard. No jumping or laughing or swinging? That didn't sound fun at all! Treelo decided it was time to talk to Ojo.

"It was an accident," explained Ojo.

"Ojo not mean to throw Treelo's feathers out window?" Treelo asked.

"Oh, no, Treelo," said Ojo. "I would never throw your feathers out the window. I'm really, really sorry."

Treelo nodded. "Treelo sorry too," he said. "Treelo not mean to get mad and run away."

And then Treelo and Ojo ran off to find some new feathers for Treelo's collection.

"Happy feather hunting!" called Bear.

Back in the living room, Bear found Tutter and Pip and Pop playing with Clammy. Tutter pushed Clammy's button.

Clammy laughed his crazy laugh. "Hey, I'm Clammy!" he said. "Dig me, baby, dig me!"

Tutter laughed. "Great Gouda, that's funny!" he said.

Suddenly, Tutter turned to Bear. "Push my head," he said.

Bear did.

Tutter did his best Clammy impression. "I'm Tutter the mouse. *Cheesed* to meet you."

Everyone howled with laughter.

Next Tutter pressed Bear's head. "I'm Bear," Bear said. "It's *beary* nice to meet you!"

Everyone laughed even more.

"I guess we're all feeling a little silly!" said Bear.

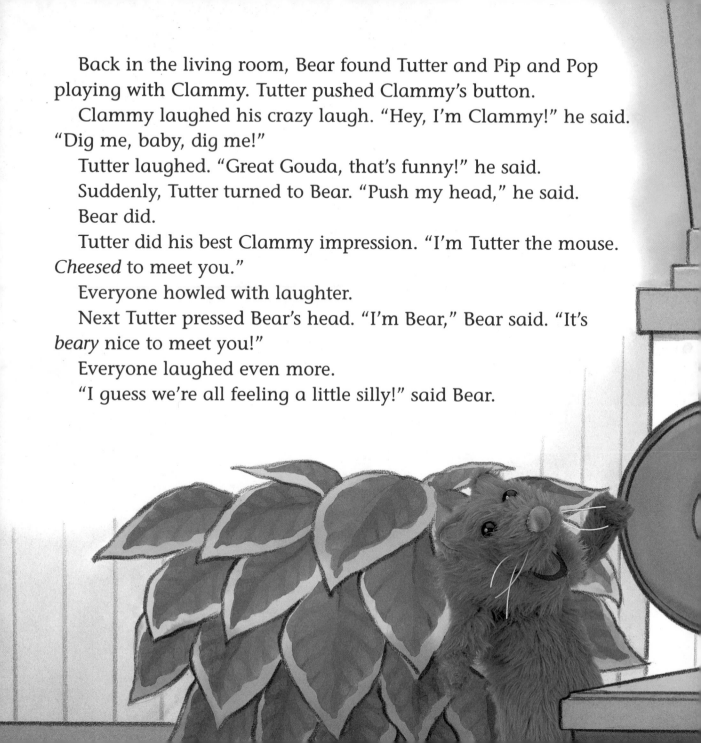

What a day it had been at the Big Blue House! Bear's friends had felt happy, sad, mad, worried, and silly.

"You know how I feel right now, guys?" asked Bear.

"How?" everyone wanted to know.

"Well," Bear said, "I have the best friends in the world and that makes me feel . . ."

"Joyful!" said Ojo.

"Glad!" said Treelo.

"Cheerful!" said Pip and Pop together.

"Delighted?" asked Tutter. "Am I right?"

"You're *all* right!" said Bear. "And what a wonderful feeling it is."